U0152242

書　　　名	《茂學・峰雋》
編　　　輯	《茂學・峰雋》編輯委員會
出　　　版	佛教茂峰法師紀念中學
製　　　作	超媒體出版有限公司
地　　　址	荃灣柴灣角街34-36號萬達來工業中心21樓2室
出版計劃查詢	（852）3596 4296
電　　　郵	info@easy-publish.org
網　　　址	http://www.easy-publish.org
香港總經銷	聯合新零售(香港)有限公司
版　　　次	二零二二年十月初版
圖書分類	流行讀物
國際書號	978-988-8806-22-5
定　　　價	HK$68

序

　　我校一向秉承「明智顯悲」校訓，推行佛化教育，啟發同學智慧，培育他們善良及慈悲心，並貫徹優良的關愛文化及卓越的訓輔教育，為我們的莘莘學子提供愉快及和諧友愛的學習環境，以培養同學高尚的品德情操及正確價值觀，將來成為良好的國民。

　　「學習、育才、展能」是學校重要的功能，因此我們會努力育才樹人，為學生製造機遇，展現他們豐碩的學習成果，成就學生踏上青雲路，成為未來社會的棟樑。

　　《茂學・峰雋》收錄了我校近年學生優秀的英文、中文寫作及視覺藝術作品，為他們創造「展能」的平台，讓同學之間砥礪切磋，見賢思齊，並藉此表揚學生傑出的表現。同時，希望與各位分享同學的作品、創作的心路歷程及喜悅，各位的支持及鼓勵將會是同學們成長的重要原動力。

　　我們會致力提供優質的教育，讓同學精益求精，盡展所長，敬希得到各位的鼎力支持。

目錄 |

|目錄

視藝科

目錄 |

中文科
學生優秀作品

友誼讓世界閃閃發光
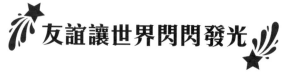

2A　黎桂宇

　　她就是我的光，我的救贖，把我從一個深淵裡拯救出來的希望。她很漂亮、很溫柔，有白皙的皮膚，有一雙清澈的雙眼。她對我很好，會在我失落的時候安慰我，在我做錯事的時候，她會給予我無數的包容、寬容和關愛。她對每一個人都很和善，但對我，會比別人更好，對我來說，她就像是一顆閃亮的星星，在我的世界裡閃閃發光，照亮了世界裡無數個陰暗的角落。

　　我曾經情緒異常低落。在那段時間裡，我一直不願與別人交流，也不出房門，連父母也無計可施。我的性格變得孤僻，經常感到煩躁不安，對所有事物失去了興趣，甚至失去了生存的動力，我變得不再像是我自己。後來我被人排擠。但唯獨她，不會像別人一樣嘲笑我，也不會孤立我，反而一直安慰我。

　　我一開始，和她只是普通同學，但她對我，就像是認識了十多年的朋友一樣，在別人欺負我的時候會幫助我，在我被嘲笑的時候，她會叫別人住口，並且會因為別人嘲笑我而感到生氣，但我還是對她冷言相向，因為我認為沒有人會想

和一頭「怪物」成為朋友。如果和「怪物」成為朋友，就會被別人孤立和嘲笑。

但她完全不認為我是一頭「怪物」，甚至對我就像是家人一樣，後來，我和她更變成了好朋友……

在一個平常的日子裡，嘲笑我的人在我進課室的時候說：「早上好呀，怪物！」但我已經習以為常，並不會為了這句話而生氣，但在我身後的她不一樣。在平日裡，對所有人都有禮貌和友善的她，因為那些嘲笑我為「怪物」的人而生氣，並和他們吵了起來，她跟我說：「那些人真的很壞啊！怎麼可以三番四次地拿別人來開玩笑，難道看見別人痛苦就是他們的快樂泉源嗎？」

小息時，我跟她說：「你和我這頭怪物一起玩而被別人孤立，為什麼還要和我一起玩？」她就說：「我從不認為你是一頭怪物，你很好，不要因為他們的幾句說話而質疑自己。」我有點震驚，她就像一顆星星，不但照亮了我的世界，還讓我慢慢地產生了變化。

我在她每天的開導下，思想也變得積極起來，回想起她對我說過的一句話：「惡意就是這樣，無緣無故地針對一個

人,即是別人沒有做錯什麼。」這句話在當時給了我很大的安慰,她就像一束光照進我的世界,雖然她只是一個普通人,但在我心目中,她就像神明一樣,無時無刻都給了我希望,照亮我的世界。

「世界很大,總會遇到一個照亮你世界的人。」哪怕是一段簡單的友誼,也能照亮一個人黯淡無光的世界。

> 創作是一個不斷尋找靈感的過程,我的創作靈感來自於我的夢境。我的夢裡,有一個少女經常被嘲笑,每天都生活在陰暗裡。後來出現了另一個少女,她的出現為少女帶來了光,在光的照耀下,少女慢慢變得開朗,這時候,夢醒了,我把夢境記在腦中,在紙上寫下我的夢。

鼓勵讓世界閃閃發光

2C　嚴紫柵

甚麼讓世界閃閃發光？我認為是鼓勵讓世界閃閃發光，說一番鼓勵的話，或無聲的支援都可以鼓動很多人，想起「鼓勵」，我想起了一件令我難以忘懷的事情⋯⋯

我小學的時候，五月份，臨近考試，我開始緊張起來，因為我怕自己考得不理想，成績差，於是我一直努力地溫習。

但是某天下午放學的時候，老師找我，我以為是自己作業寫得不好，低著頭走了出去，可是老師卻沒有責備我，反而說：「我看得出來，你因為考試，心情緊張，我不是來責備你的。」然後，老師叫我坐在他的旁邊，老師說：「臨近考試了，放開往日學習中的緊張，用一顆平常心去應對，相信你會考出自我夢想的成績，你要相信自我，對自我有信心，努力吧，考試順利！」老師一直在鼓勵我，他說的話深深地觸動了我的心靈。完成考試後，成績發了出來，我不負眾望，拿了理想的成績，我很感謝那位老師。

還有一次，我聽聞一則故事，有一位女士因重症住院，情況較為嚴重。她聽見醫生說明病情後，就痛哭了起來，傷

心欲絕。但她的家人和朋友請她不要放棄治療，那名女士的家人說：「孩子，誰都難免會遭遇病魔的侵襲，但我們相信，好好治病，你能戰勝病魔，贏得勝利！我們永遠都在愛著你，支持你！」她的朋友附和說道：「要注意身體，多喝水，早點恢復健康，我相信你能戰勝病魔，願我的朋友早日康復，一天天好起來，等著和你一起去遊玩呢！」一直鼓勵那名女士。說來也很奇怪，那名女士一直很失落，不願意治療，但聽見家人和朋友的鼓勵，就聽取了建議，堅定地接受治療，在治療的期間她一直保持樂觀，她的家人和朋友也一直陪著她對抗病魔，也一直鼓勵她，三個月後，她竟然比預期中更快康復，整個人變得活潑開朗，臉色也很好，身體也很健康，真是不可思議。

　　寫到這裡，我又想起了小時候的一件事，在我六歲的時候，媽媽送我一輛非常漂亮的自行車，它全身都是粉色的。我很喜歡那輛自行車，媽媽說：「買了它，就要學會騎它。」我立即爽快說：「好！這個自行車看起來那麼簡單，肯定不難學。」看我輕鬆的神情。媽媽又說：「那你騎上去試一試，它沒有那麼簡單學會的。」媽媽話音剛落，就聽到「砰」一聲，我從自行車摔到地上來。媽媽就在一旁鼓勵我：「堅持練習！你可以的！」然後我忍著要流下來的眼淚，繼續練習，但這次又因為沒有掌握好平衡，又摔到地上，我忍不住

了「哇」一聲哭了起來，我心情又傷心又氣憤。媽媽連忙扶我起來，溫柔地摸了摸我的頭髮，鼓勵我說道：「世上無難事，只怕有心人。為什麼遇到一點小小的困難就哭了？」我在心想：是啊，只要用心學，就一定會成功的！於是，我連忙擦乾眼淚，在媽媽的鼓勵下，經過一個下午的艱苦練習，我終於會騎自行車了！

　　成長路上，我學會了很多道理，在生活中，面對困境，我們可能會有走投無路的感覺。可是，仔細看看周圍的人，父母、老師和朋友，都會在我們無助的時候鼓勵我們，不要氣餒，堅持下去！他們堅定地在向前走著，他們變成了閃閃發光的存在。原來一番鼓勵的話，或無聲的支援都可以鼓動很多人。如果大家都在別人沮喪失落之時，送一句鼓勵或讚美的話，就能讓他感到陽光的溫暖，讓他知道在茫茫人海中他不是孤獨的，一直有人在關注著他，與他同行。所以，我認為鼓勵可以讓世界閃閃發光。

　　每個人都希望在垂頭喪氣的時候，突然有人站出來鼓勵他、安慰他。既然這是我們輕而易舉，而能給原本灰心喪氣的人帶來希望，那為何不做呢？人生就像星空，永遠都找不到方向，慶幸有無數星光指引。

　　我一直覺得，別人失意的時候要對其多加鼓勵。鼓勵是一種良好的教育方式。

　　無論這個世界怎樣對你，人們都應一如既往的努力、勇敢、充滿希望。因為心有所期，全力以赴，定有所成。

微笑讓世界閃閃發光

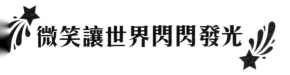

3C　黃善怡

　　微笑是冬日的陽光，溫暖人的心靈；微笑是淡淡的清風，輕輕拂去心靈的塵埃；微笑是黑暗中的明燈，能感染別人的心情；微笑使人的心靈不再陰暗，令世界閃閃發光。

　　微笑讓人不再懼怕。桑蘭在紐約友好運動會上意外受傷。她從小立志做一個體操選手，卻沒想到這場意外，奪走了她的活動能力。令所有人意料不及的是，桑蘭沒有放棄，沒有被生活的難關所嚇倒，她笑著面對困難，她是一個愛笑的女孩，遭受如此重大變故卻堅毅不屈，從不抱怨，總是笑著面對。終於，皇天不負有心人，現在的她站在殘運會上的領獎台，向大家訴說她的故事，一邊笑著一邊說，桑蘭的故事令不少自卑的人都重新振作，笑著面對生活，她的笑容融化了不少失意人心中的懼怕，微笑確實讓世界閃閃發光。

　　微笑讓人歡樂。泰國商人施利華在一次的金融危機中破產，面對如此重大變故，他先是沉默，然後再哈哈大笑。「哈！哈！哈！好啊！又可以重新來過了。」之後市面上多了一間公司叫「微笑有限公司」。公司的標語是：「今天你微笑了嗎？」沒錯，這所公司正是施利華開設的。有不少人

看到這公司名字都不禁哈哈大笑呢！施利華之後還開了微笑貧窮基金、微笑建設公司、微笑小學等等⋯⋯他的公司越開越多，在世界各地都不難看到他的分店，而施利華的目標也只是叫大家多多笑，少皺緊眉頭，哈哈大笑才是正確做法。他的做法，他的心態，值得我們學習。他讓大家都微笑起來，微笑確實讓世界閃閃發光。

微笑能感染人心。在日常生活，有不少人會煩惱、會傷心、會生氣，但只要一個笑容，甚或壞的事情都能拋諸腦後。在醫院，醫生護士與丈夫都在為準媽媽打氣。「加油！加油！」「嗚哇！嗚哇！」嬰兒出生了！媽媽抱起了嬰孩，嬰孩笑了，媽媽也笑了，大家也笑了。球場上，一方輸了比賽，觀眾大叫可惜，突然，一名隊員大叫：「我們一定會再回來的！」隨之哈哈大笑起來，全場不禁一邊鼓掌，一邊大笑，微笑確實讓世界閃閃發光。

可能很多人在想，為甚麼他們的人緣、運氣、做事都能事事如意？因為他們笑啊！他們笑，所以他們成功了，如何讓世界閃閃發光？你的微笑、你的笑聲會讓世界閃閃發光，所以，朋友你今天笑了嗎？

　　微笑能為自己增加自信、微笑能給人帶來快樂、微笑能使世界更美好。希望大家不要吝嗇一個簡單的微笑，用自己的笑容感染一個又一個的人。我相信定能為失意的人重新振奮，為傷心的人治療心靈，為快樂的人更快樂。就讓微笑成為我們生命的風帆，把正向的力量傳遍開去，讓世界閃閃發光。

生活中的菩薩

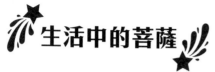

4D　彭仁曼

　　小時候帶著「留守兒童」的稱號，與爸爸媽媽長期分開，我們一直被遙遠的地區分隔，天各一方。日復一日，年復一年，每天都期待著再見一面，每天都過著想念爸爸媽媽的日子。猶幸，我有一個很疼愛我的奶奶，像菩薩一樣默默守護著我，伴我渡過整個童年。

　　奶奶她視力不太好，眼皮也因為年齡的增長變得下垂、鬆弛，眼周布滿皺紋，皺紋彷彿是飽經風霜，嚐盡人間疾苦的見證，然而這些皺紋卻顯得她格外溫柔。仔細看，奶奶的眼睛呈「八」字形，好像總睜不開似的，小得不知道她有否睜眼。奶奶總愛將花白的頭髮盤成髮髻，在我眼裡卻是十分老氣。我很少看到她換穿其他款式的衣服，她總是穿著碎花圖案的上衣，可能生活在農村的緣故，奶奶擁有的衣服也很少，即使髒了也不常替換。總之，奶奶整體的感覺就是老氣。

　　不過奶奶從不對我吝嗇，總是給我最好的。我小時候很任性，記得有天在地上撿到一張麥當勞的廣告宣傳單張，宣傳單張的食物惹人注目，令人垂涎三尺，裡面的雞腿漢堡包是它們家的招牌，也是最吸引我的。我抱著期待雀躍的心情馬

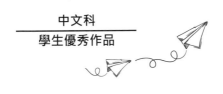

上拿回家給奶奶看，叫她做給我吃。到家後，我把宣傳單張展示在奶奶面前，用手指指著雞腿漢堡包。可是，農村裡哪有這些食物呀，別說吃了，奶奶看都沒看過，根本不知道這是什麼。我試著用手比劃一個雞的圖案，她好像懂了，知道我說的是雞，我便放心離去，對奶奶炮製的食物滿懷期待。

第二天晚上，飯桌上擺著一隻被煮熟的雞，還未被斬開。看到這，我愣住了，這和我預期的，想要的，完全不一樣。我兇狠地瞪著奶奶，她好像沒有察覺我的眼神和心情，照舊在我的對面坐下，盛飯給我，然後第一時間把雞最滑、最肥美的雞腿扒開給我，遞到我面前。下一刻，我發怒了，我把整隻雞摔到地上，飯碗、雞與地板激烈碰撞，發出「砰砰」聲，地板上一片狼藉，奶奶好像被嚇到了，我卻顧不得奶奶，摔門而去。

晚上，農村地曠人稀，途人寥寥無幾。抬頭一看，夜空滿目繁星，偶然還會有些蟬蟲在唱歌，我想著：爸爸媽媽在城市，應該看不到如此美景吧，真慶幸自己跟了奶奶生活在農村，但一想到奶奶的老氣落伍，心中的埋怨又油然升起……

「咦！曼曼，你在這裡幹什麼呢？」一把熟悉的聲音傳來，是住在附近的阿姨。我們的關係還算好，有時碰到還會

聊幾句。我黑著臉回答道:「我不想回家,不想吃奶奶做的飯。」明慧的她猜到我剛剛和奶奶發生了點爭執,說道:「你這樣把奶奶一個人丟在家,她會很孤獨,而且我昨天還看見她一大早,彎著背,攀山涉水去捉一隻雞回來,是為了你吧?」

我瞬間好像明白了什麼,想到了奶奶的眼睛和膝蓋都不太好,一個人攀山涉水去捉雞是很困難的,卻為了我去冒險。我說想要什麼,她便給我什麼,對我總是有求必應,奶奶對我的愛早已超越父母,腦海裡與奶奶的回憶不斷上湧⋯⋯在更小的時候,我被住在附近的小霸王欺負,哭著跑回家,說要找那個小霸王報仇。她看到我哭得淚流滿面,淚珠不停地往下掉,就會抱起我,安慰著我,幫我擦掉臉上的淚水。她說做人要大度,人之所以充滿煩惱,就是沒有自在的心,仇恨和執著只會讓人活得更加痛苦,要我放下執著,學懂原諒,我就會活得更加通透,最後奶奶教會我兩個字 ——「慈悲」。她如菩薩一樣教導我道理,指引我走向正確的道路。還有一次,我被附近的惡狗吠叫聲嚇得大聲哭喊時,也是奶奶第一時間趕來救我,令我免受侵害,使我在危難中得到援助。奶奶與菩薩一樣,她愛我,卻從不會跟我說,只是一直在背後默默守護著我,給予我無限的愛護。想到這些,明白到奶奶的愛是如此珍貴,原來我一直擁有許多居住在城市的小孩沒有的,我卻渾然不知,我真愚蠢!我匆匆向阿姨道謝

後，便立刻跑回家，打算向奶奶道歉。

　　剛打開家門，我就看見奶奶在屋裡收拾剛剛的殘局。她彎着背，瞇着眼，用鬆弛、滿佈皺紋的雙手去執拾地上的飯菜時，讓我感到更加心痛和愧疚。

　　「奶奶……」我先開口，她聽見是我的聲音，停止了收拾，轉過身來望向我。「曼曼！你剛剛跑去哪了？可把我擔心死了，你還未吃飯吧？我切了點西瓜等著你回來吃呢！」她說這番話的語氣尤其地溫柔，我衝上前抱住她，哭著說：「對不起，奶奶，我剛剛不應該這樣對你。」這句話看似老土沒有誠意，但千言萬語也道不盡此刻內心的愧疚和自責。沒想到，她摸著我的頭，邊跟我說：「沒關係，人誰無過，錯而能改，善莫大焉。沒有人不犯錯的，只要犯錯後能夠改正，就是莫大的善事。」說完，她流露出慈悲又善良的笑容，像菩薩一樣，她一次又一次的慈悲待我，使我心靈上得到救贖，這使我更堅定奶奶是我心裡的唯一菩薩。就算我再不聽話，她仍會以無盡的愛包容我，即使遇上我的惡言惡行，仍然充滿智慧、善巧地將問題化解，她時刻擁有一顆清靜的心，有她在的家才算避風港。

　　我邊吃著奶奶切的西瓜，邊看著奶奶打掃、洗碗。看著她微微郁動的背影，我喊了一聲：「奶奶，怎麼了？」她轉身望向我。「沒事，就想說有您真好！」我們相視而笑，快樂的笑聲彌漫整個屋內。

　　「家家彌陀佛，戶戶觀世音」，每個人的生命中都會有一個菩薩，你也許未能察覺，但她常在你的左右，會令你在危難中得到援助，難過時使你安心，也教會你慈悲待人，使你心靈得到救贖。奶奶在家裡給予我平安，只要我有所求，她便如觀音菩薩滿足我所願。她的懷抱是我唯一的避風港，是任何時候我都可以依靠的地方。奶奶對我來說就是菩薩的化身，她是我生命中最常在的菩薩。

　　願我能在日常生活中實踐六度四攝，盡力協助需要救助的人，解決他們的困難，分擔他們的憂苦。願我也能成為別人生命中的菩薩。

　　我創作這篇文章的靈感是來自於我曾經在網上看過的留守兒童和空巢老人的生活影片。人人都說留守兒童的世界是灰暗的，在成長階段裡，他們缺少父母的陪伴，性格有缺陷，甚至造成自卑。我卻不這麼認為，父母雖然缺席了他們的成長，但他們家裡卻有很好的老人陪著他們，他們的陪伴填補了爸媽的那一部份。他們也是被愛包圍長大的孩子。他們更懂得感恩，心中同樣有愛，也有一顆慈悲的心。

　　希望大家對留守兒童不要留有刻板印象，不要認為他們都是缺乏教育的壞孩子。也希望人們明白觀音菩薩處處都在。

今日發生的事情，至晚上仍歷歷在目，更讓我深刻領悟到佛學課上所學的因果業報

5D　黃靖

今日發生的事情，至晚上仍歷歷在目，更讓我深刻領悟到佛學課上所學的因果業報。世間萬物都是偶然出現的嗎？過去、現在及未來的一念之差，總在冥冥之中就像萬有引力般，互為因果，招感個人乃至一個家庭的業報。

「勇兒……你不能這樣對我。」清靜的樓道間，蕩漾著隔壁王阿婆的哀嚎聲。平日溫和的婆婆怎麼恍惚間性情大變？我拉開半掩著的門，瞧見對門的兩個身影。

「當年，妳拿走了我爸的救命錢去賭博，應該想到會有今日。」眉眼間與阿婆神似的男子音量拔高，眼神遊走，似乎在尋找著某樣東西。

「我知道從小到大你對我的成見很深，你爸死後的這些年，我……我也深刻意識到自己的過錯，我不應該去賭，我知道錯了。」王阿婆拼命攥緊兒子的左手，殷切地盼望得到原諒。

中年男子發出冷笑：「妳現在跟我說，知錯了，有什麼用？我爸能活過來嗎？」話語間，他順手拿起桌上的相框，高舉過頭頂，打算順勢一摔。

「不要扔！」王阿婆大喊，「你要什麼我都能給你，除了那張相片。」沉默了半晌，男子緩慢地放下相框，突然冒出一句：「二叔當年送給爸的懷錶在哪？拿完我就走。」

老人家聽聞即刻回屋，許久，她的身影再次出現在我的視野中，手裡擦拭著某樣物件——正是男子口中很重要的懷錶。「能不能讓我見一見孫兒？就把他接過來住幾天……」

男子從老人家手中奪過懷錶，音量提高了幾分：「不可能。」玄關處傳來一陣匆忙的腳步聲，接著歸於一片平靜。

自我記事起，王阿婆就住在我家對門。在鄰里眼中，她是位性格古怪的長者，總是獨來獨往，也沒人瞭解她的過去。那年清明節前，我回家時看見王阿婆提著數個膠袋，艱難地爬著樓梯，於是順手幫了她一把，此後她便對我特別熱情，間中邀請我去她家坐會兒，陪她聊天，平日她也總是送糕點去我家，一來一往，兩家人也就熟絡了起來。

　　可是，年輕時候的王阿婆曾沉迷賭博？這怎麼可能，雖然婆婆從未提及過去，可她多年來一直是獨居，家中電器皆是十幾年前的款式，平日最喜獨坐窗邊，一坐便是兩、三個鐘，總是注視著遠方，好像在盼望著什麼，亦不曾見有親朋好友登門拜訪，怎會是中年男人口中的「好賭之人」？我佯裝出門散步，想邀阿婆一同前往，卻被她叫住。「孩子，想必你都聽到了。」老人家緩緩坐下，並道：「你過來坐。」

　　「婆婆年輕時做了很多錯事，一時沉迷賭博輸光了身家，心生貪念，竟鬼迷心竅，拿丈夫的治病錢繼續賭。」老人家低頭愛撫著那張對她來說彌足珍貴的相片，淚珠在眼眶中打轉，順著眉睫滴落，打濕了相片上笑容璀璨的三口之家。「現在婆婆經歷的一切不過是在償還當年的債，妳可千萬別像婆婆這樣，一定要遠離那些貪念……」夕陽的餘暉灑在她身上，暈染出金色的輪廓，為她平添幾分落寞之感。

　　眼前的種種，讓我憶起佛學課上「業報與輪迴」。眾生因為被無明與煩惱所障蔽，常有人為了世間短暫的名利、錢財、幸福快樂，而做出種種愚痴的行為，以致種下惡因，招感惡報。《正法念處經》曾記載：「非異人作惡，異人受苦報；自業自得果，眾生皆如是。」每個人的命運並不是冥冥之中有主宰，更不是無緣無故偶然發生的，而是受自己的作業所

牽引和束縛，現在的結果何嘗不是受過去的行為所影響呢？王婆婆的「一念之差」，鬼迷心竅步入不歸之路，無形之中種下惡因，受業力牽引，愛人、家人相繼離開，餘生被「苦」束縛，無法享受天倫之樂，何其痛苦。

世人總是要對自己的行為負責任，此乃因果業報的法則。凡夫的所作所為，無不是由慾望驅使的結果，貪念本身沒有善惡之分，只是不容易得到滿足，倘若過度放縱，反而會演變成罪惡的種子。佛法中所謂的「緣起性空」，意即一切法都是眾因緣生滅而沒有自性，如果能生起這種智慧，覺知世間萬物隨緣而聚散，隨業而流轉，家與親人，皆依附著「緣起」而暫時存在，又依據因緣果報而消散，那麼是否能讓彼時的念消散？婆婆的親人相繼離開，並不是永遠消失了，不過是換一種方式，跟隨因緣業力繼續流轉。過去的行為造成今日的一番境遇，已成定數，絕非人力能改變，但當下的行為卻依然由自己的心決定，我們往往被外在的事物牽引著內心，鮮少能沉靜下來了解事物的真正面貌，一念之差，能為未來培育出幸福快樂的種子，也能成為一生痛苦的束縛。何不及時修身、修戒、修心，改變自己的心意，化慾望作為修行，業報或能隨之而改變。

「如果當年，我未曾心生貪念，及時回頭，是否便不會是今日這番景象了？」王阿婆把相片擁入懷中，留下懺悔的眼淚。

　　在這個世界上發生的所有事情，一定有前因後果。人們往往因為一時的過失，帶來負面的業報，讓自己陷入無始無終的痛苦，但其實都是徒勞無益，何不讓自己的心安定下來，通達本性，煩惱自然也會煙消雲散。

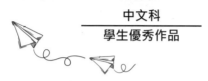

逆行者是永遠的光亮

5D　黃靖

　　庚子鼠年伊始，新冠疫情來勢洶洶，夜深人靜之際，有一群「逆行者」轉身離開，「明知山有虎，偏向虎山行」。落下的太陽總會升起，逆行者作為每個時代的「提燈人」，在危險中書寫著家國情懷和滿腔赤誠，照亮漫漫前路的曙光。

　　回望泱泱華夏，早在上古時期，「神農嘗百草之味，一日而遇七十毒」，為黎明百姓帶來生命之光；後有「逆行者」明代李時珍不怕山高路遠，不畏酷暑嚴寒，周遊列國自創《本草綱目》一作，福芸芸眾生。先人們懷大愛無疆的精神，在歷史長河中留下一行行逆行的腳步，就像暗夜中的光明使者，喚醒沉睡的靈魂，指引世人不斷追尋。

　　多年前，天津濱海新區某倉庫內危險品意外爆炸，當所有人失措不安，一心只想著逃離危險之境時，數位消防員義無反顧地逆行進入火場，甘願陷入水深火熱之中，救他人於黑暗，從此「逆行者」家喻戶曉。何來「歲月靜好」一說？不過是有人在負重前行。「最帥逆行者」奮不顧身衝進火場，他們只是心懷眾生的平凡人，身上閃耀英雄的耀眼光環，他們早已將生死置之度外，在火光中逆行，實現生命的獨特價值。

　　抗疫之路漫長而顛簸，前有八十五歲高齡的鍾南山院士，帶領青年醫護工作者多次深入重疫區，秉承「捨我其誰」的擔當精神；後有新生代的新聞工作者主動請求去往救援站，用紙墨書寫一個又一個不同凡響的事跡；更有熱心市民自費購買幾百個口罩，放在警局門口後悄然離開，以一己之力詮釋何謂「捨棄小我、成全大我」的無私奉獻精神。誰說只有偉大人物才能發光發熱？古往今來，華夏民族一直向大眾傳遞「不破樓蘭終不還」的決心，我們之所以每逢天災都能安穩度過，從來不是因為有傳說中的救世主，而是在災難來臨前，總有千千萬萬個普通人挺身而出，打破無盡黑夜，保家衛國，展現直擊靈魂深處的震撼力量，仔細看，他們身上閃著人性「真、善、美」的光亮。

　　星星的光芒雖然微弱，但它永遠都不會黯淡，那銀白色的天河如若少了它，將是虛無。我們應該去發光，而不是等待被照亮。也許「逆行者」對大多數人而言，意味著遙不可及的奉獻精神，我想，「逆行」是追光，亦是追夢，許多職業看似尋常，卻在不同崗位上熠熠生輝。「天下興亡，匹夫有責」，作為新生健兒的我們，也可追尋前輩的腳步，成為抗疫志願者，於社區內派發防疫物資，向居民普及防疫知識，為社會福祉做貢獻，在網絡平台為「逆行者們」打氣，以吾輩之力為華夏民族再添無數濃墨重彩！

疫情讓「逆行者」的概念深入人心，他們並非天賦異稟，卻共有一份心懷國家百姓、心繫天下民生的慈悲心，他們散發的光彩是生生不息的，而我們更應該在這光芒照耀之下，敢於尋找屬於自己的光明。

你，願意成為「逆行者」，照亮他人嗎？

> 被疫情的陰霾，無情籠罩著的幾個春夏秋冬中，世人總是擔驚受怕，卻有一群人迎面朝著黑暗及危險的方向前進 —— 醫護、義工、科研人員等堅持在抗疫一線的工作者。我才發現原來從古至今，總有許多「平凡」的人，他們一直在做著不平凡的事。

今天發生的事情，至晚上仍歷歷在目，更讓我深刻領悟到佛學堂上所學的「不忘初心，方得始終」

5D　楊穎精

今天發生的事情，至晚上仍歷歷在目，更讓我深刻領悟到佛學堂上所學的「不忘初心，方得始終」，我終於理解到為何佛門常說「發心如初，成佛有餘」，也明白為何我們不能被貪嗔痴所蒙蔽。風吹過我，又吹往窗，像是引領我看萬家燈火，街道上車水馬龍，緩緩墜入回憶的深淵。

「啪噠」一聲在空曠的溜冰場縈迴着，勸告着我的失敗。這個跳躍動作我練習了無數次，經歷了數不盡的失敗，對的，一次也沒有成功過。我忍着疼痛扶着冰面站了起來，身上仿似負重千萬噸重石，手上黏着一點冰碎，壓着手掌，有點冰冷，也有點疼痛，但更為冰冷的卻是我的內心，令我疼痛的是付出努力卻沒有得到回報。

我滑到教練的面前，有點不甘地對他說：「教練，我想換比賽的動作，我不跳三周跳了，可不可以換成那個我每次跳都成功的跳躍動作。」他的臉像被山嵐遮掩了般，我不清

楚他在想甚麼。頃刻，他緩緩開口：「不換了，繼續練。」我着急地解釋道：「雖然那個動作分數不高，但如果三周跳失敗了就要扣更多分了！」他依然示意我繼續練習。我無法理解，把多次練習失敗的委屈通通渲泄出來，「再不成功完成跳躍我就無法取得金牌了！無法連勝！那些曾經的輝煌通通都會被質疑的！」我哭着向教練大吼着。教練沉默了，沉默像是冰刃，但沉默下有更殘忍的話語刺痛着我「你剛學花樣溜冰的時候就說要完成三周跳，說這是你的目標，現在你卻為了成就背叛了擁有初心的自己。」他說罷就離開了冰場，留下了我獨自面對那些頹坦敗瓦。

我按了按心臟處，好像停了一拍，又如雷般的跳動，巨大的疼痛與失落接踵而至。我無力地癱坐在地上，觸碰着我視為信仰的冰面，翻覆地思索着剛才教練的話。我看向遠處，白茫茫的溜冰場上空無一人，朦朧間我彷彿看到了小時候的自己，不斷練習着同一個動作，那是我現在已經練得滾瓜爛熟的動作，但對當時的我來說是一個天大的困難。那時候的我跌倒會再次站起，教練問道：「要放棄嗎？」然後目光堅定地回答：「不！我要繼續練，我愛溜冰！長大後還要跳到三周跳！」對於花式溜冰的熱愛已經十年了，甚麼時候那份熱愛枯萎了，一片只有利慾的荒漠了呢？當年的目標和初心甚麼時候被成就齧噬掉呢？現在的我放棄了當時的初心，反而

向那些虛無的名利屈服，原來我早已背叛了當年那個清澈如水的自己。

　　我癱坐在冰面上，感受着四方八面的風。我思緒混亂得像漿糊一樣，頭痛得無法制止，一些回憶碎片衝擊着我的大腦，我捕捉了其中一塊，我想到了佛學堂老師曾說，若要平靜思緒，並非要強制自己停止思考，而是應該靜下來，聽聽那些思緒與內心在向自己訴說甚麼，而禪修的四念住會使我們的覺察更敏銳。於是我閉了雙眼，開始了一場禪修，風向我吹來，風中帶着冰面上的碎冰，使我感受到寒冷，甚至有一點刺骨，我覺察到現在身體的冰冷和過去那些舊患在停止運動時的痛楚。我一步一步接近自己的內心，我覺察現在的自己不是真正的快樂，我正被那些功名與成就所纏繞着，我也感受到眼淚緩緩地從眼角落下。我呼了一口氣，再沉寂自己，我在內心看到了曾經快樂溜冰的自己，也看到對成就執迷不悟的自己，那些功名把我的初心淹沒了，我嘗試把那些功與名撥開，想起那時最純淨的初心，我覺察到利慾並不能使我進步，我不該把功名看得那麼重，反而應該要好好平衡成就與初心，好好比賽，但不要忘記比賽的原因是測試自己的水平，讓自己更加精進，而非只重視名利。

　　我緩緩張開眼睛，風繼續吹着，我整個人因四念住而變

得清醒，禪修過後我想到佛學課上聽到一句話：「每天醒來時請把昨天的自己當作死去的人，今天的自己不是重生，而是一個全新的人。」小時候聽到此話，還沒能參透當中的意思，我還故作聰明地對他說：「明明我們都是被時間所囚禁的三維生物，昨天死了哪有今天的我呢？」他只是笑笑不說話。而今天的我終於明白了，在人來人往的物質社會和被欲望吞噬的價值觀，清澈如水的初心和目標會是率先被蒙上一層氤氳的東西。世事紛紛擾擾，我們都很容易被貪嗔痴所損害，對成就的過份偏執，對失敗的過份抗拒，對勸喻的不理解，漸漸地早已忘了自己的初心是甚麼，總是執著於過去所得的名利，認為名利應要一次比一次大，逐漸地我對自己越發不滿，不斷折磨現在的自己，但其實我們應要放下過去的榮辱得失，每一天都當成是全新的一天，把自己當成是全新的人，不要被過去的成就所影響，在初心和目標中找到努力的意義。

我再次站了起來，今次身體好像因自己的覺醒而變得輕盈了，往日因成就而帶來的重擔彷彿已經消逝，留下那重新找回的初心。我沿着溜冰場滑着，溫柔的風與我擦肩而過，我伸手輕撫着風感受速度與那些熱愛，我彷彿聽到那時候的我說：「還要挑戰多次嗎？」這次換我堅定地回答：「無論還要經歷多少失敗，我的回答都會是『我要挑戰』。」我乘

着風躍起，在空中旋轉三周，然後單足下地，但重心不穩，扶了一下冰面，但我滿足地笑了。

　　晚風輕輕拂過我的臉，我躺在床上看着窗外，今晚是月色皎潔的靜謐春夜，我承載着那份初心合上眼睛，期待明天全新的自己。

　　寫作時正值 2022 北京冬運會。在男子花式滑冰項目中，羽生結弦選手的表現與體育精神令我印象深刻。我觀看他的訪問後，更被他渴望精進的精神與不忘初心打動，令我想起佛學所學到的理論，成為我創作此文章的靈感。

家燈是永遠的光亮

5D 楊穎精

「本次列車馬上進站，請下車的乘客做好準備……」冰冷的女聲傳入耳中，刺激着我的神經線。我睡眼惺忪地張開眼睛，凝望窗外的萬家燈火，心想不知那燈光也是否在等待着誰。看着明暗不一的燈光，忽然與腦海中某一個回憶聯繫。我想起了那束家鄉的光亮，那束溫暖的光亮，那束在我心中永遠的光亮——家燈。

我家在農村，那裡只有熱心村民為夜讀學生安裝的幾柱街燈，而那些街燈也只會發出暗淡的昏黃，這裡是名副其實的「燈火闌珊處」。可是就在這暗淡無光的農村，卻有一束永遠的光芒，那是我家的燈光。

那時我快要考大學，每日在學校完成溫習時，天色早已被黑暗吞噬，四周寂寂無光，昏黃的光把我的影子拉得很長很長，一種對孤獨和黑暗恐懼的人性本能逐漸浮現，但我抬起頭望向遠方，家燈發出明亮的光芒指引着回家的路，身邊的一切仿似突然明亮了，我向家燈的方向大步踏去，這束光彷彿是我生命唯一認定的光。

「咔」我打開了門，婆婆聽到聲音後，從廚房拿着一碗熱湯緩緩地走出來。她站在燈光下被裹上了一層柔和，仿似是溫暖的源頭，使人想靠近。每次我都會跟婆婆說：「婆婆，那麼晚了你還不睡，我要考上大城市的大學，要溫習到很晚才回來，你早點睡。」婆婆每次聽到都只會笑笑，然後溫柔地對我說：「這不是因為你還沒回來，我擔心嘛，不要緊的。乖，來喝湯。」婆婆和家燈好像無論天多麼黑，時間怎樣流逝，他們都永遠不變地等待我回家，為我送上溫暖。

後來，我成功考上城市的大學，看到了城市繁華的街燈，它們照耀了那些想飛黃騰達的心，照耀那些少年的夢想，卻未能照耀那些孤獨思鄉的心。再後來，我自己在市區居住，打算挑一盞燈作為家燈，但好像無論什麼款式，什麼顏色的燈泡都沒有家燈那盞燈那麼明亮和溫暖。我想，大概是因為沒了那個為自己開燈的人吧！

列車停止前行，思緒也跟隨列車停止，我收拾好行裝匆匆下車，大步地踏上回家的真正路途，就像小時候那樣看着家燈大步地走着。我想，家燈之所以重要，不只是指引歸家者回家的路途，而是給予他們一種被等待的希冀，讓他們知道原來家中仍有人在等待自己，仿似對路途上疲累的歸家者說了句：「或者我無法為你做什麼，但我仍在你身邊。」

在黑暗裡替歸家者掛上一顆閃爍的指路星；在冰冷的道路添上溫暖和愛，照耀歸家者對孤獨的恐懼和黑夜的悵然。

　　瞳孔逐漸縮小，明亮的家燈在我眼前發着光芒，我踏進家門，一個熟悉的身影徐徐地走出廚房，站在家燈下，就仿似昔日一切也沒有變化。婆婆依舊溫柔地對我說：「我特意把燈提早開，怕你看不見回家的路，來！吃飯吧！」熱湯的氤氳攀上眼鏡，眼淚悄然地滑過臉頰，「婆婆！我好想你！」我哽咽地道。婆婆笑笑地說：「傻孩子，只要你想回家，婆婆永遠都在，家燈也永遠為你而開。」

　　有人說，時間就像流水會把回憶和愛沖洗得像鵝卵石一樣光溜溜。然而真正愛你的人無論如何都會敵過時間，總會在你困倦的時候為你開一盞燈，總會陪你走過那些漫長苦悶的悠悠歲月，總會抹走那些含糊濡濕的誤會，然後擁抱你。

　　天是一樣的天，風是一樣的風，但家裡的光無其他地方能及，家裡那份溫暖無其他地方的能敵。家燈是永遠的溫暖，家燈也是永遠的光亮。

　　故事背景的靈感來自修祥明先生的《小站歌聲》，故事中純樸的情感令我感動，因此希望以鄉村背景，突出人與人之間除去物質之外的情誼。創作靈感源於本人的童年，婆婆會開著家中的燈，等待晚歸的父親回家，並為其送上一碗熱湯，由此聯繫到〈家燈是永遠的光亮〉。

夢想是永遠的光亮

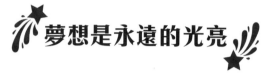

5D　羅嘉文

　　人生路漫漫，許多路都是自己走的，時常會形單影隻，但夢想會永遠在人的心中，宛如一道光，在你面前，照亮你前進的道路；在你身旁，無聲地陪伴你；在你身後，替你驅散黑暗，永遠照亮着你。

　　被國際乒聯稱為「不可能先生」的哈馬度，表示出戰勝里約殘奧是他的夢想之一。由於哈馬度在十歲的時候遭遇火車意外，失去雙臂，使他一度灰心喪志，也因此被玩伴取笑，認為他永遠都不能再打乒乓球。不過，正是因為這些話激起他的鬥心，令他重拾人生意義——打乒乓球，為國爭光。失去雙臂的他需要比別人多付出時間及要更有決心，就算在練習時遇到困難，但因心中有夢，仍然咬牙堅持，不斷地挑戰自己，最終以口持拍，以腳發球，走上里約殘奧，成為乒壇奇景。他用實際行動，印證了老話「以夢為馬，以汗為泉，不忘初心，不負韶華。」夢想是在人們面對挑戰時，就像黑暗中的路燈，照亮夜色，為你增添一份前進的信心。

　　夢想不單給予支持及動力，還會在人沮喪的時候，支撐、溫暖着你，給你帶來光亮。梵高在經歷多次受挫後，找到了

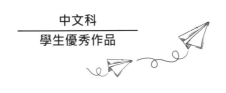

影響自己一生的夢想——繪畫，為此他不停地繪畫，向名師求教，儘管遭遇拒絕，亦從未想過放棄；儘管畫商不願售他的畫，他仍繼續作畫，不斷完善繪畫技術。只因夢想給予他前進的動力，給予他希望和光亮，使他雙眸不再灰暗。就算他的生活仍困頓不堪，自己也因患上癲癇病而被送進精神病院，但都沒有阻止他對夢想的追求和創作的熱情。他從不抱怨生活的艱辛，只因他有摯愛的夢想，最終他的繪畫從最初的灰暗無光慢慢變得光明有色彩。

馬雲曾說過「沒有夢想比貧窮更可怕，因為這代表着對未來沒有希望。」而有夢想的人知道自己想要什麼，不在乎他人的看法，堅持到最後。有「光纖之父」之稱的諾貝爾物理學獎得主高錕教授，他的夢想是希望未來人們可以免費上網，而他在提出光纖理論時，並不獲外界認同，還被批評「癡人說夢」，但因為有夢想，他不害怕路上被荊棘刺破褲腳，劃傷皮膚，仍然繼續研究，取得成就。高錕教授曾寄語年輕人應如他一般要有夢想，努力實踐，總有成功的一天。夢想猶如太陽般，不停照耀着我們，就算在我們看不到的地方，亦一聲不響地陪伴我們。

前人用畢生的經歷告訴我們夢想如同親情，永遠在無形之中支持，陪伴著你，而世上最幸福的事，莫過於徹底了解

自己的人生夢想，由於夢想會在人的心裡閃閃發光，使人積極、樂觀、向上進取，夢想是永遠的光亮。

> 失敗、自責、嘲笑都會使我一步步陷入自我懷疑、放棄的無底深淵，但夢想，它給我前進的動力，就像無窮的力量，在背後推動我，在前方給我光亮，一步步指引我爬出無底的黑洞。

All about Myself

1C   Lok Cyrus

Hello! I am Cyrus. I am twelve years old. I study in Buddhist Mau Fung Memorial College and I am in Class 1C. You are welcome to view my blog and leave comments.

About myself

I live in Yuen Long. My favourite drink is apple green tea. My favourite food is spaghetti. It is very tasty. My favourite sports are playing basketball and badminton. It is healthy to do sports often. I like dogs and hamsters, too. They are cute.

About my school

My school is very large. It has seven floors. I like the library at my school because I can read many books after school. I go to the library with my friends. My favourite subject is English because I like reading English books and listening to English songs. I have three class teachers. They are Mr. Yeung, Mr. Leung and Ms. Kwok.

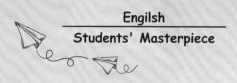

Mr. Yeung teaches me Math. Mr. Leung teaches me Buddhist Studies. Ms. Kwok teaches me Chinese History. They are strict but interesting.

About my new friends

One of my new friends is Harvard. He is fourteen years old. He is tall and handsome. Although he is very clever, he is lazy. His favourite person is Iron Man. His favourite animals are squirrels. They are adorable. He likes playing basketball very much. He often plays basketball on the basketball court after school. Also, he likes Thai food very much, especially lettuce with shredded meat.

About my hobbies

I like playing basketball. I always play basketball with my friends. It is fun and wonderful. I also like playing games on the phone. I always play games with my friends. It is enjoyable and exciting.

Well, I want to make friends. Could you tell me more about your lifestyles or anything interesting? Write soon and all the best.

This article is written by Cyrus Lok from 1C. As a new student of Buddhist Mau Fung Memorial College, he introduces himself comprehensively, including his hobbies, his school and his new friend he has made at this school. Good to know you better! I can foresee that you will have a beautiful life at Buddhist Mau Fung Memorial College!

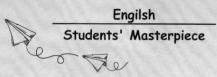

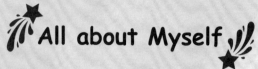

All about Myself

1C Sit San Yim

Hello! I am E-yen. I am twelve years old. I study in Buddhist Mau Fung Memorial College and I am in Class 1C. You are welcome to view my blog and leave comments.

About my school

My school is in Tin Shui Wai. It is very huge. It has seven floors. I like the music room at my school because I like playing the piano and it is interesting. My favourite subject is P.E. because I like running. I have three class teachers. They are Mr. Yeung, Mr. Leung and Ms. Kwok. Mr. Yeung teaches us Mathematics. Mr. Leung teaches us Buddhist Studies. Ms. Kwok teaches us Chinese History. They are strict but helpful.

About my new friends

I have a friend, Hailey. She is twelve years old. She is very beautiful. She has a lively, cheerful and optimistic personality. She likes to eat fruits such as durians and apples. We like walking on the street and playing volleyball together. Hailey's hobbies are playing the piano and guitar. She likes cats, too.

About my hobbies

I like playing volleyball. I always play volleyball with my friends. It is fun and interesting. I also like playing basketball. I always play it with my friends. It is exciting and amazing.

Well, I want to make friends. Could you tell me more about your lifestyles or anything interesting? Write soon and all the best.

This article is written by Sit San Yim from 1C. As a new student of Buddhist Mau Fung Memorial College, she likes her school so much. Therefore, she is eager to share her amazing school life and her new friend she has made here. If you have a chance to see Sit San Yim at Mau Fung, don't forget to say hello to her and she will be very happy with it!

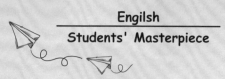

A Letter of Advice

2B Cheung Kwok Hin

Dear Kitty,

Thank you for your email. I'm sorry to hear about your problems and that you feel stressed and lonely. Don't worry. I can give you some advice to help with your problems.

First, you said that you should do sports, for example, basketball, football and volleyball. Doing sports is a good way to keep fit because it can help us burn calories. You may feel very tired after doing it the first time. It's normal. If I were you, I would take a break and drink some water. You should feel much better after the break.

You also mentioned that your classmates always call you names and you feel stressed and cannot stop eating junk food. You should ask your teacher for help. If your classmates call you names, your teacher will help solve the problems.

If you're under stress, you should reduce your stress. First, you can do anything you like to make you feel very happy. If I were you, I would listen to music, play computer games, meet my friends and read books. Also, you must have to try your best to control yourself. I understand it is very hard for you to stop eating junk food. You can try eating healthy food like vegetables, green peas, sweet potatoes and natural potato chips. They are healthy and yummy.

Finally, you want to tell your parents about your problems but they are very busy. If I were you, I would use the apps like WhatsApp to communicate with my parents. You can also join some school clubs to meet some new friends so you do not feel lonely. I hope my advice can help you. See you.

Best wishes,
Hennessy

> This letter is written by Cheung Kwok Hin from 2B. As a teenager, Hennessy realizes many youngsters face different challenges and difficulties such as study, family, peer or even health problems. He understands these and tries to provide with some practical advice in this letter. You will know how warm-hearted and considerate Hennessy is. If you have any problems next time, Hennessy can be a good listener and is willing to give you some advice!

A Letter of Advice

2C Lee Shing Ying

Hello again, Kitty!

In your latest email, you mentioned that you and your family lack communication. That must be hard for you to bear. I can't imagine the despair when your family ignores you. However, maybe we can fix this problem? I thought of a few suggestions for you.

First, you should try to tell your family members how you feel about the situation. If you feel nervous about talking, you can always write a sticky note or a letter to put on your parents' or siblings' bedside tables. It's easy for them to notice. I'm sure that they will talk to you after that.

Another suggestion of mine for you is to join more activities with them. If I were you, I would spend some quality time with them. In that way, they will notice you and be more willing to listen to your problems.

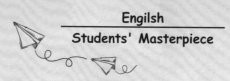

These are my suggestions. You can always ask your teachers or friends for help. Find out which advice you feel the most comfortable with and act on it. I hope you find a way to solve your problem! Good luck!

Yours truly,
Angel

This article is written by Lee Shing Ying from 2C. In the article, Shing Ying sees from the viewpoint of Kitty, who suffers from family problems, and provides practical advice to her. She shows the readers the maturity and sensitivity of a teenage girl in nowadays' society.

A Letter of Advice

2C Zhang Pui Yee

Dear Kitty,

Thank you for your email. I'm sorry that you're feeling helpless. It can be tough being a teenager.

First, you mentioned in your email that you had nowhere to study. I know that you are annoyed because your siblings are always fighting. Let me give you some advice. First, you should find a quiet place to study. Then, you should create a study place at home. Finally, if I were you, I would talk to the teacher, parents and social workers about your problems so that they can help you solve your difficulties.

Second, you mentioned in your email that you had poor communication with your parents. I know that you are frustrated because you have nobody to talk to in the family. Let me give you some advice. First, you should talk to your social worker about your problems. Then, you should give them calls frequently so that both of you have

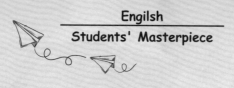

time to chat. If I were you, I would try to ask my parents to spend quality time with me. Going for a picnic together is a good choice for you to enhance your communication within the family.

Finally, you mentioned in your email that you had money problems. I know that you feel anxious because you spend a lot of money on buying unnecessary stuff. Let me give you some advice. You should think clearly when buying things. Then, you should control yourself. If you go to buy something that is not urgent, don't buy it and you can save more pocket money. If I were you, I would find some part-time jobs like working in a convenience store to earn some extra money.

Good luck! I'm sure things will get better soon.

Best wishes,
Chris

This letter is written by Zhang Pui Yee from 2C. As a friendly and understanding girl, Emma is always on your side and supports you. Therefore, she suggests a number of useful advice in this letter to solve Kitty's problems. We don't know if Kitty's problems can be settled finally. However, I think she can feel the warmth from Emma and is glad that there is a good companion with her!

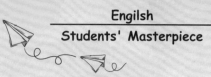

Book Review

3A Leung Hoi Lam

Charlotte's Web is a fantasy fiction written by E.B. White. The book tells us about the story of Wilbur who is very loyal because it protects Charlotte's children.

In the book, my favourite character is Charlotte. She is helpful and smart. Charlotte uses its magical net to resolve the survival crisis of the little pig Wilbur. She establishes a deep and firm friendship with Wilbur. Also, since Charlotte uses the magical net to help Wilbur, Wilbur escapes the fate of being slaughtered and is able to stay alive.

Therefore, for me, Charlotte is a helpful and smart character.

This book report is written by Leung Hoi Lam Leanna from 3A. The language used is concise and the report is well-organized. Leanna effectively shares with the readers a reflection on one of the Classic children's books—Charlotte's Web.

A Charity Day

3A Yeung Wing Kei

Today, the weather was warm and sunny. Our school held a charity day. I participated in a jumble sale and a charity concert on that day. I also bought snacks and ate with relish.

In the afternoon, the charity sale began. I saw all kinds of toys, learning aids, books for leisure reading and many other goods. It also had different supplies. I saw a box of puzzles at the first sight and I couldn't wait to buy it. I saw a brand new pencil box at the second sight and I immediately bought it. After the sale, the teachers and I donated our old clothes. I also heard that our school received more than 3000 items of second-hand clothing and got more than 10,000 dollars. I was very happy.

The concert was held in school at 6 pm. I heard someone scream and the concert began. We picked up our stools and ran to the playground. I was a little bit sleepy when I was listening to the music. I lowered my

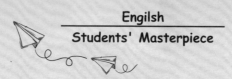
head quietly and a pleasant song broke all the silence. I looked up and saw that it was Alan. Alan is a top singer in my class. I listened to his nice song and I thought it was so interesting. After listening to the music, we got some book coupons. I donated them to the charity.

The charity day was interesting. It was a great experience. I hope everyone will get involved in charity events.

This is an article written by Yeung Wing Kei from 3A. The article allows Wing Kei to fully unleash his creativity and imagine himself being a participant in a charity event. By reading the article, readers can be able to experience the day from the perspective of a creative and warm-hearted teenage boy.

A Charity Day

3D   Chan Ho

Last weekend, our school held a jumble sale at the school hall from 12:10 to 13:20. It was an event to raise money for Greenpeace to plant trees in Hong Kong. As a school student, I was invited to participate in the event.

On the day of the event, all students and teachers were involved. The school hall was filled with excitement and laughter. There were a lot of things we could buy, such as books and stationery. I bought some canned food. It was yummy and very cheap.

It was a day of non-stop fun! It was the most interesting sale. Over 10,000 dollars was collected to help plant trees in Hong Kong. I hope we have another jumble sale next year and raise more money!

"
This is a piece of short writing written by Chan Ho from 3D. Chan Ho plays the role of a participant in a jumble sale and shares with readers his joyous experience in this event. It is an informative article that includes the essential information about the activity and some of the original ideas from the writer.
"

A Letter of Advice

4A Cheung Sze Yiu

Dear Taylor,

Thank you for your letter. I'm glad to hear that everything is going well. Sorry I'm a bit late in replying because I've been busy with my schoolwork. I'm so happy to hear that you will have a job interview for the position of Cultural Ambassador. I understand that you feel a little nervous about this interview. Don't be scared. Here are a few tips to help you.

Before the group interview, try to review all the information you can find about the company. Also, you could get a few friends to role-play a group interview with you. Before you attend the interview, try to find out as much as you can about not only the job, but also the company. Company research is important for interview preparation. It will help you prepare to answer interview questions about the company. You should allow enough time to get there. It's fine to arrive 15 minutes early. Bring the phone number of your interviewers just in case

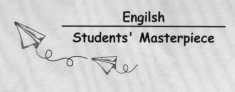

you get lost or are going to be late. If you are going to be late, call to let the interviewers know.

During the group interview, you should make eye contact with everyone. Do not dominate the interview. Listen to others attentively when they speak. Be yourself and be trustworthy. Be polite and greet everyone you meet. When you enter the interview room, offer the interviewers a warm greeting. These first few seconds can give a good first impression to the interviewers. At the end of the interview, don't forget to thank the interviewers for giving you the opportunity for the meeting.

I hope the above advice helps you prepare well for the interview. Be positive and confident. Hopefully your interview will succeed and don't forget to let me know about the result.

Best wishes,
Chris

This letter is written by Cheung Sze Yiu from 4A. We may attend different interviews related to study or job after we graduated from secondary school. However, what things can we prepare and pay attention to in advance? If you are worried about this and want to know more, Sze Yiu's advice can help you for sure. You can find some practical suggestions in the letter and become a wise interviewee!

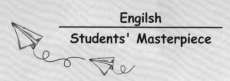

The Pros and Cons of Undergoing Plastic Surgery

5A Wu Yat Long

Nowadays, cosmetic surgery is becoming more and more popular among young people. The rising tide of cosmetic surgery has aroused extensive public discussion. Many people undergo cosmetic surgery to pursue a perfect appearance. Some people try cosmetic surgery because they are dissatisfied with their original appearance. But if you fail the plastic surgery, your appearance will be damaged forever.

There are a lot of advantages of undergoing cosmetic surgery. First of all, one of the benefits of undergoing cosmetic surgery is that cosmetic surgery helps people with low self-esteem and self-confidence. For example, some people are uglier than others, which makes them lack self-confidence. But after cosmetic surgery, they can regain their confidence because they become more popular. Second, it is generally believed that cosmetic surgery helps people get more job opportunities. For

example, a salesperson of beauty products is a job that pays great attention to the appearance of the person, so getting a perfect appearance can help you find a job. Third, one precious gain credited to cosmetic surgery is that it helps people who suffer from accidents or who are born with defects. For example, some people are born with strange features, such as birthmarks, so they need cosmetic surgery to fix them. Cosmetic surgery can change their lives. Also, I think cosmetic surgery can change people's destinies, make people live a normal life and become more popular. They are all the advantages of undergoing plastic surgery.

Still, there are some disadvantages of undergoing cosmetic surgery. First of all, one of the drawbacks of undergoing plastic surgery is that cosmetic surgery involves high cost. Why does cosmetic surgery involve high cost? It is because cosmetic surgery is quite expensive. Why is cosmetic surgery expensive? It is because cosmetic surgery typically lasts for 10 years and the results from Botox, for example, last for about 3-4 months. You need to pay more if you do cosmetic surgery more than once. In addition, if the cosmetic surgery

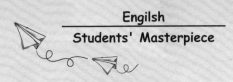
fails, it will leave permanent scar and you need to spend more money to recover. Second, cosmetic surgery has a negative impact on psychological health. For example, if you fail the cosmetic surgery, you will be discriminated against by the outside world. Also, if you make an imperfect appearance, this will make you lose confidence and you will avoid people. Finally, cosmetic surgery causes people to run the risk of being infected, disfigured or even paralysed. It is because cosmetic surgery is not 100% successful, so it causes facial paralysis. After all, the whole operation is always risky.

It is high time we understood the advantages and disadvantages of cosmetic surgery. It is hoped that we must think twice about doing cosmetic surgery before we act.

This article is written by Wu Yat Long from 5A. He discusses the rising trend of undergoing cosmetic surgery. However, what are the pros and cons of this social phenomenon? You will have more understanding of it after reading this article.

My Views on Building a New Amusement Park in Hong Kong

5B   Lui Tsz Him

Dear Editor,

I am writing to express my opinions on building a new amusement park. It is because Ocean Park and Disneyland are extremely boring in Hong Kong. Both of them are family-oriented. We are fed up with all those old games. There are no other choices of theme parks we can go to. I do believe Hong Kong should build a new park for young people who want thrilling, heart-stopping rides.

I suggest that the government should build a Ferrari-themed park. It mainly targets teenagers. In the theme park, you can ride on a Ferrari roller coaster with a speed of up to 250 km/h in 4 seconds. It will be the fastest roller coaster in the world. People will cross the finishing line feeling like a true Scuderia Ferrari champion. It is crazy for teenagers to experience the most state-of-the-art roller coaster in Hong Kong.

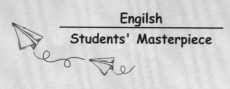

As we know, Ferrari is a renowned brand recognized worldwide. Building this Ferrari-themed park benefits Hong Kong a lot. It can boost tourism, create endless job opportunities, increase Hong Kong's range of entertainment options and enhance Hong Kong's image as an exciting travel destination.

To sum up, I strongly agree that the government should build a new amusement park in Hong Kong.

Yours faithfully,

Chris Wong

This article is written by Lui Tsz Him from 5B. Many Hong Kong people are not able to travel overseas under the pandemic. It is a chance for us to build a new amusement park in Hong Kong in order to let us release our pressure in daily life. Tsz Him suggests some interesting and creative ideas about the theme of the new park. I will visit it at once if it becomes real on day!

About the Pros and Cons of Undergoing Cosmetic Surgery

5B Ngan Lit Ching

Nowadays, cosmetic surgery is a billion-dollar business. There is a strong influence from the mass media and it has a powerful impact on teenagers in Hong Kong. It is observed that many famous Korean celebrities have undergone cosmetic surgery in order to get fame. Thus, people have accepted cosmetic surgery as part of the culture. The burgeoning popularity of cosmetic surgery has stirred up heated discussion among people. With the advanced technology, people want to change their appearance and enhance their beauty. However, it is not surprising that there are many serious incidents while undergoing cosmetic surgery in private clinics and beauty parlours.

There are lots of benefits when having cosmetic surgery. First, cosmetic surgery is not just to make a person's appearance more beautiful, it can increase one's self-confidence and boost his or her self-esteem.

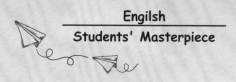
Beautiful people tend to get more free gifts and better services when they buy things. They make a better first impression on other people and are promoted faster in the workplace. Research shows that beautiful people get more job opportunities than average-looking people because they look more trustworthy and reliable. That's why you will find many beautiful people in the top management of international companies. Also, there are people who really need plastic surgery. It is because they were born with a physical defect or those who have scars or deformations due to accidents. It may be a good chance for them to enhance their appearance. Cosmetic surgery can help them live a normal life.

Regarding the disadvantages of undergoing cosmetic surgery, it may be potentially dangerous. If the operations are done by unlicensed doctors or dishonest therapists who simply want to make money, cosmetic surgery may lead to severe and damaging consequences or even death. Unsuccessful cosmetic surgery can ruin a person's life. Also, people who go under the knife usually have some psychological issues. They will never be satisfied with their appearance. They may blindly chase to have multiple cosmetic surgeries to achieve beauty perfection. Cosmetic surgery is ridiculously pricey. People may go into traps that lead them to have huge monetary debts. Finally, they are sucked into an endless cycle.

All in all, cosmetic surgery can change oneself. But it also brings certain risks. Cosmetic surgery can only change what's on the outside, but not the inside. The most important thing for a person is inner beauty and beauty mostly comes from within. Having good personal qualities makes a person beautiful, considerate and caring. Moral conduct and manners are very important. So, undergoing cosmetic surgery is unnecessary as one's personalities, manners and abilities are far more important than physical appearance.

This article is written by Ngan Lit Ching from 5B. Undergoing cosmetic surgery becomes more and more popular nowadays. Most people are obsessed with beauty. However, what are the hidden risks behind this? Other than beauty, what characteristics should we have to achieve whole-person development? You will have more understanding of these after reading this article.

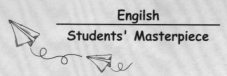

How Much Do You Know about Cosmetic Surgery?

5D Shih Min Chung

Nowadays, cosmetic surgery is one of the most popular operations in the world. You may see advertisements of cosmetic surgery anywhere, anytime. It is no doubt that cosmetic surgery is becoming increasingly popular. The rising tide of cosmetic surgery has aroused extensive public discussion.

Why is cosmetic surgery so popular? This may be a question many people will be asking. There are some reasons that make cosmetic surgery so popular. First, people have cosmetic surgery to be more confident. Some people are not satisfied with their faces or bodies. They want to change their appearance. Therefore, cosmetic surgery is their sole choice as it can make their faces and bodies beautiful. Because of this, people can enhance their self-esteem. Second, people have cosmetic surgery for more opportunities. Some people may be discriminated against

by others because of their ugly appearances. They get fewer job opportunities. After cosmetic surgery, people can give a better impression to others.

However, cosmetic surgery is quite risky. Unsuccessful cosmetic surgery can ruin a person's life. In recent years, there have been many reports of cosmetic surgery procedures which have gone wrong. These procedures were done by unlicensed doctors who used drugs that do not meet specifications. They simply wanted to make more money so the cheap drugs are their best options but most of the drugs do not meet specifications. The off-specification drugs may cause permanent nerve or organ damage, or disfigurement. Also, there are many surgeries which are performed in unhygienic environments. This is extremely dangerous for people because of the large number of bacteria. It may result in bacterial infection during the operation.

I do not suggest people undergoing cosmetic surgery. Everyone has his or her own appearance. It is the most natural and unique. If you undergo cosmetic surgery, you will become the untrue you. Therefore, please don't be silly. It is not wise to have cosmetic surgery.

> This article is written by Shih Min Chung from 5D. Min Chun in the essay brilliantly provides with readers some real-life evidence to argue against the notion of undergoing plastic surgery. This informative essay shows his in-depth understanding of the issue and his critical mindset.

My Views on Building a New Amusement Park in Hong Kong

5D Yeung Wing Ching

Dear Editor,

I am writing to express my views on building a new amusement park in Hong Kong. Currently, there are two amusement parks in Hong Kong, Ocean Park and Disneyland, but they still can't accommodate too many tourists and lack new elements. Therefore, it is necessary to build a new one.

It is recommended that the government builds a theme park about the movie called 'Charlie and the Chocolate Factory'. In view of the popularity of this film, people will love this place. Also, 'Charlie and the Chocolate Factory' is popular in Hong Kong too. If there is a theme park, it must be able to evoke collective memories of Hong Kong people. About the rides, we can restore some scenes in the movie, for example, Charlie's house and 'The Chocolate Park'. Imagine if the movie becomes the reality, how do you feel?

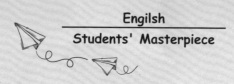

About the potential benefits of the new park, it can attract more tourists to come to Hong Kong. The movie is very famous internationally, but other countries do not have this theme park. Therefore, it must be able to attract many tourists to visit and spend money. Thus, it can promote the development of Hong Kong's tourism industry and consolidate Hong Kong's international tourism position.

Also, this theme park can promote Hong Kong's economy since it requires a lot of labour to operate such as cleaners and staff members. It will create more job opportunities. Therefore, building a new theme park can help reduce Hong Kong's unemployment rate and promote Hong Kong's Gross Domestic Product (GDP) to achieve higher economic growth.

The above is my opinion. I hope the government will accept it since it is helpful to Hong Kong's development and tourist position. Thank you for your consideration.

Yours faithfully,
Chris Wong

Students' Masterpiece

"

This letter to the Editor is written by Yeung Wing Ching from 5D. Yeung adopts the cinematic element from the 'Charlie and the Chocolate Factory' and suggests building a Chocolate Factory as the new amusement park in Hong Kong. The letter implies not only her creativity, but also her acceptance of different cultures.

"

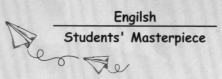

Students Are Stressed

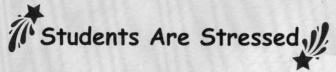

6A Yan Wai Laam

Academic stress coupled with the ongoing epidemic leads to the significant increase in students' stress and anxiety levels, and some students are even reluctant to go to school. Let us look at this issue now.

Some students are stressed because they have too much homework. They may have to spend more than three hours each day doing their homework. Students may not have enough time to do other activities. So, they can't relieve the stress and may not have enough time to relax. As a result, they build up stress. Their mental development will be affected.

However, we should help students relieve their stress. Firstly, students should make time to do other activities. For example, some students like to play basketball, some students like to listen to music, some students like to eat etc. These can help relieve stress. In addition, students should talk to someone when they are stressed, such as friends and family.

To sum up, some students are stressed because they have too much homework. Also, they should learn to relieve stress.

This article is written by Yan Wai Laam from 6A. Yan in her writing indicates some possible factors causing academic stress during the COVID-19 pandemic and useful ways to ease the pressure. As a student who has also gone through such hardship, the article is undoubtedly a genuine sharing of her personal experience and feelings.

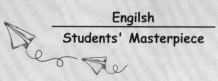

The Champion of Friendship

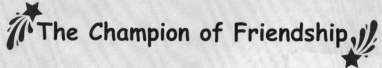

6D Muhammad Ismail

It was a typical sunny day in the forest. Birds were chirping happily, flowers were blooming and squirrels were busy finding food. It was the time of spring. Here came the hare making its way among the bushes. The hare groaned, "What a boring day! I have no one to play with and nothing to play." As he was groaning, something fell on his head. It was a leaf printed with the words, "Join the first race and win a mysterious grand prize." The hare looked at it for a while. "Well, it could be fun to try," he thought. He rushed to Mr. Lion, who holds this race, to show his interest. What the hare did not know was that he needed a partner for the race. When he did, he was angry and shouted, "Where am I going to find a partner this late?" Mr. Lion exhaled, "You'll find someone. Go and find someone or you'll not be able to join the race." After that, the hare got tensed and ran to find a companion for the race.

The first person he thought of was Mr. Leopard, the fastest animal in the forest. The hare approached him, "Mr. Leopard, can you join my team for the race? You can run as fast as a lightning bolt. I could really use your help!" Mr. Leopard signed, "I wish I could but you see I have a wound on my leg and I can't run until summer." The hare was disappointed and went away. He encountered Miss. Snake, the hare asked her, "Can you join me in the race? I bet you could wiggle through the obstacle quickly." Miss. Snake apologized, "I am really sorry. I just agreed to Mr. Kangaroo's invitation. You should have come to me earlier." The hare got more and more frustrated and he did not even notice when he walked past the tortoise, who was calling out in a tiny voice, "Um...do you want to join the obstacle race? We can team up." The hare looked back, "What? You?" the tortoise nodded. "But you run too slow. Who would want to join the competition and just run slowly?" the hare laughed. The tortoise was not angry or disappointed. He went forward "Well, that's just because you haven't discovered my talents." The hare was still not convinced. He saw the time and the sun was about to set down. With no one else as a partner, he reluctantly agreed

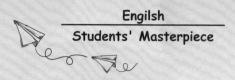
to the deal and went to apply.

Everyone who participated in the race started to train themselves. Everyone wanted to win the mysterious prize.

After a long-awaited week, it was time for the race. Everyone gathered at the starting line. The hare woke up late, but he got to the point on time. He started to find the tortoise. He found him behind the tree stretching. The hare giggled after seeing it, "Are you seriously stretching? You can't run very fast." The tortoise smiled and replied, "We'll see about that." The hare got irritated after hearing this.

The time has come. The contestants were ready to race. They took their marks. As the whistle blew, the hare left everyone behind and rushed to take the lead. He was indeed a talented athlete. Behind him, Mr. Kangaroo tripped over his own legs while leaping around and the spines of the hedgehog brought down every twig he passed through. How ridiculous was that? None of these affected the hare. He ran and ran until he reached

the first obstacle of the test, the lake.

Normally, hares can swim but little hare has never swum before. He stared desperately at the flowing water. His competitors were starting to catch up with him and jumped into the lake one by one. "Oh no, I am going to lose!" he murmured. The animals were going very slowly in the lake. "H-hey, hare! Wh... what now?" The tortoise panted. The hare saw him in shock. "Tortoise? You are really speedy by the standard of tortoises!" "I have been practicing for weeks," the tortoise smiled, "Why don't we jump into the water? It must be cool!". "I...I haven't tried swimming before," the hare stammered. The tortoise gave a crispy laugh and then crawled into the lake in no time. "Come climb on my back," the tortoise insisted. The hare was unable to utter a single word. He settled himself on the tortoise's back. Thanks to the swimming skills of the tortoise, they crossed the lake in no time, even faster than the others. The hare cheered, "We are in the lead!". "We need to run faster if we want to keep it," the tortoise added.

Soon, they arrived at the second obstacle. This time,

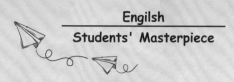

they needed to jump over a large fence and rushed through the mud. "How are you going to get through the fence?" the hare worried. "Calm down," the tortoise replied with a smile, "My shell will be a little platform for you so you can jump over the fence." The hare hopped onto the shell. He jumped as stiff as he could. He jumped over the fence. The hare tensed, "What about you?". The tortoise started to use his brain. He was digging to make his way through. "Smart move!" the hare complimented. The tortoise and the hare worked together and left everyone behind. They got to the mud. The tortoise stood on it using its big feet. The tortoise gave a look to the hare and the hare understood what he meant. He jumped onto the shell then onto the other side! After that, the tortoise just simply walked through. The hare praised, "I didn't know you had some great talents! If I did not team up with you, I would never get this far." The tortoise didn't say anything and smiled. The hare smiled back. They finally got together.

Only 100 meters left. The hare and the tortoise were still in the lead. Even the hare, a fast runner, did not complain about the tortoise's speed. He was impressed by the tortoise's wisdom and calmness. Together, they

passed the finishing line. Mr. Lion, the judge of the race, told them, "You guys are the first group to finish the race." "We won!" the hare jumped up and down. Slowly, other participants finished the race one by one.

It was time to give out the mysterious prize. Mr. Lion took it out. It was shining in the sun. It was a diamond in the shape of a star. The hare and the tortoise were shocked to see it. "It's so beautiful," they said together. They were very pleased. The tortoise smiled as he always did, "I think we won more than the diamond." The hare puzzled, "What else did we win? You won the champion of the day." Seeing that the hare was still confused, the tortoise added, "You won the champion of friendship." The hare smiled back.

The hare and the tortoise were best friends after this race. They helped each other out and never left each other behind, but always had the back of each other. I hope that everyone understands that everyone has talents. We just need to acknowledge it. We need friends. Friends are the ones who always help you. We need a friend that will come out to help us no matter what when we are in trouble.

This is a story written by Muhammad Ismail from 6D. It talks about a competitive hare that ridicules a tortoise at first but then befriends it after cooperating with the tortoise in a race. Muhammad Ismail cleverly adapts the "The Tortoise and the Hare" in Aesop's Fables and successfully produces a richer story, which gives readers a new insight.

Engilsh
Students' Masterpiece

曾詩宇 (1A)

昆蟲樂園 (版畫)

文依敏 (1A)

昆蟲樂園 (版畫)

以「樂園」為主題，創作一幅單色凸版畫。

陳思穎 (1B)

昆蟲樂園 (版畫)

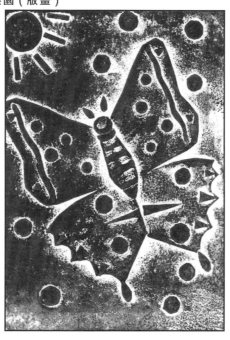

楊思翹 (1C)

動物樂園 (版畫)

何琳 (1D)
奇異的水果 （繪畫）

陳家琳 (1D)
奇異的動物 （繪畫）

林明健 (1B)
奇異的昆蟲 （繪畫）

梁芷琪 (1D)
奇異的花卉 （繪畫）

以「點、線、面」為創作元素，加入豐富想像力，繪畫一幅
獨一無二的畫作。

陳熹洋 (2E)
大象在神秘的極光下休息（繪畫）

趙梓丞 (2E)
貓與主人在神秘的極光下嬉戲（繪畫）

賴佳蔚 (2E)
駱駝在神秘的極光下漫步（繪畫）

莫佩鈺 (2E)
小鹿在神秘的極光下走著（繪畫）

以鄰近色及明度色彩原理，繪畫極光效果作為背景。加入人、動物或大自然剪影圖像，展現出在神秘極光下的活動情境。

吳雅芝 (3A)
當凱斯哈林遇上蒙特里安 (繪畫)

李泳霖 (3B)
當凱斯哈林遇上蒙特里安 (繪畫)

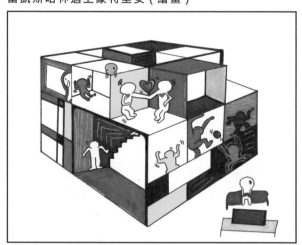

學習凱斯哈林及蒙特里安兩位藝術大師的藝術風格，創作一個創意十足的兩點透視魔方。

連晉毅 (3D)
當凱斯哈林遇上蒙特里安 (繪畫)

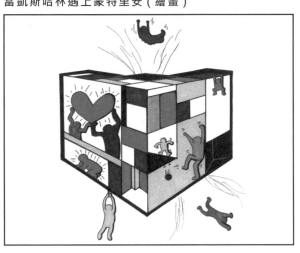

吳嘉璇 (3D)
當凱斯哈林遇上蒙特里安 (繪畫)

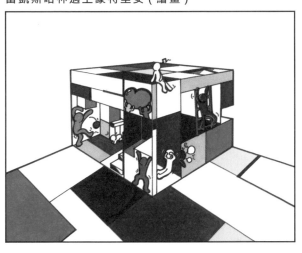

胡振光 (4B)
甜品　　　　　（麥克筆仿作）

關韻之 (4C)
甜品　　　　　（麥克筆仿作）

鍾音音 (5A)
飲品　　　　　（麥克筆仿作）

莫若希 (5B)
飲品　　　　　（麥克筆仿作）

莫若希 (5B)
風景畫 （水彩仿作）

黃嘉靖 (5D)
風景畫 （水彩仿作）

莫若希 (5B)

逃　　　　(塑膠彩)

人類的過度捕獵動物，破壞大自然生態，使得陸地及海洋裡的動物都爭相逃走保命。

黃樂詩 (6B)
夢想的女孩 （塑膠彩）

經歷人生不同階段，終於找到方向，勇敢邁向自己的理想吧！

曹寶怡 (6D)
被遺忘的光芒 (塑膠彩)

透過放大鏡展現漸漸消失的香港集體回憶，並利用現代冷冰冰的高樓大廈襯托出被遺忘的人與事。

黃樂詩 (6B)
逃出新世界 （立體創作）

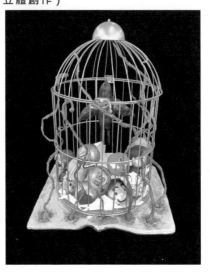

學業壓力如一波一波的浪濤。我以燕子比喻自己，希望能像牠一樣高飛著，逃離壓力帶。

陳靖文 (6B)
逃離 2020 （立體創作）

突如其來的疫情影響全球，生活從此不一樣。這一刻我只希望疫情盡快離開，回復常正生活。